This
Ready Set Read
book belongs to:

My Reading Tree!

*In memory of my
father and mother*
~ A. H. B.

*To all my friends and my
dearest wife, Tiziana*
~ J. B. B.

LITTLE TIGER PRESS
An imprint of Magi Publications
he Coda Centre, 189 Munster Road, London SW6 6AW
www.littletigerpress.com

First published in Great Britain 2002
by Little Tiger Press, London
This edition published 2011
Text copyright © A. H. Benjamin 2002
strations copyright © John Bendall-Brunello 2002

Printed in China
LTP/1800/0262/0611
ISBN 978-1-84895-365-9
2 4 6 8 10 9 7 5 3 1

Mouse, Mole,
and the
Falling Star

A.H. Benjamin

John Bendall-Brunello

I'm a star reader!

LITTLE TIGER PRESS

Mole and Mouse were
the best of friends.
They had fun together.

They shared everything.

They trusted each other completely,
even with their deepest secrets.

When one was sad
or not feeling well, the
other was always there
to comfort him.

I've an appetite for reading!

That's how much
they loved each other.
"I'm lucky to have
a friend like you,"
Mole would say.

"No," Mouse would
reply. "I'm lucky
to have a friend
like *you*!"

One summer evening, Mole and Mouse
lay side by side on top of a hill, gazing
at the starry sky.

"Aren't stars beautiful?" sighed
Mole happily.

"Yes," said Mouse, "and magic, too.
They sometimes fall from the sky, you
know. And if you ever find a fallen star,
your wishes will come true."

"Wow!" said Mole. "Then you could
wish for anything in the world, and you
would have it."

"That's right," said Mouse dreamily.
"Just imagine that!"

Mole and Mouse fell silent
for a moment, dreaming of
magic stars and all the things
they could wish for.

Just then, a shooting star zipped
across the sky! One moment it was
there, and the next, it had gone.

"Did you see that?" gasped Mole,
sitting up.

"Yes, I did," cried Mouse. "It's a
fallen star, and I'm going to find it!"

Mouse scrambled to his feet and
scurried down the hill.

"Wait!" called Mole, racing after him.
"It's my star! I saw it first."

"No, I saw it first!" shouted Mouse.
"It's *my* star!"

When they reached the bottom of
the hill, Mole and Mouse started
searching for the fallen star. Each
one hoped he would find it first.
But neither did.

"Perhaps the star fell in the woods,"
thought Mouse. "I'll go and look
for it tomorrow."

Mole stared toward the woods, too.
He was thinking exactly the same thing.

But they did not tell each other, and
they went back to their homes without
even saying good night.

The next day before sunrise, Mole snuck
out of his house and set off toward the woods
A few minutes later, Mouse did the same.

Mouse and Mole spent the whole morning
in the woods, looking for the fallen star.
Once or twice they spotted each other,
but they pretended they hadn't.

Then, toward afternoon, Mole came across a small patch of charred grass.

"Maybe this is where the star has fallen," he thought. "But someone's already taken it. It can only be Mouse!"

A little later, Mouse came across the same charred patch of grass. He thought the star had fallen there, too.

"It's gone!" he cried. "And I bet I know who's taken it. It has to be Mole!"

As darkness fell, both Mole and Mouse made their separate ways home, each feeling very angry with the other. They did not speak to each other again, except to argue.

"You stole my star!" Mole yelled.

"No, *you* stole *my* star!" Mouse yelled back.

Mole didn't trust Mouse, and Mouse didn't trust Mole.

So Mole snuck into Mouse's
house to find the star . . .

and later on Mouse looked
through Mole's window
to see where Mole had
hidden it.

But neither found
the fallen star.

The days rolled by, and summer was nearly over. Mole and Mouse grew lonely and miserable. They missed each other's company, the fun they used to have together, the secrets they had shared. They even missed the sad moments.

"Mole can keep the star if he wants,"
thought Mouse. "All I want is my
friend back."

"If I had never seen that star,
Mouse would still be my friend,"
thought Mole.

Soon the fallen star became just
a sad memory—until one day . . .

Mouse was climbing up the hill when he spotted a golden leaf, swirling and twirling in the air.

"It's the fallen star!" he cried. "Mole must have lost it. I'll catch it for him."

Not far away, Mole noticed Mouse chasing after something that looked very much like a star.

"It's Mouse's star," he thought. "I'll help him catch it."

Up and up the hill ran Mole and
Mouse, until they reached the top.
But the leaf was already high in the sky,
glimmering in the autumn sunshine.
It swayed this way and that, as if waving
good-bye, and then vanished altogether.

"The star has gone back to the sky,"
said Mouse.
   "That's where it belongs," said Mole.
   "Maybe it's for the best," sighed Mouse.
   "I'm sure it is," agreed Mole.
      There was a moment of silence.
   "Anyway, we don't need a star.
We have each other," said Mouse.
   "Of course we do," agreed Mole.

They gave each other a big hug, and then they lay back on top of the hill, feeling the wind. With their arms and legs stretched out, they looked just like two furry stars.

Picture Dictionary

Look at the words below and put the correct
picture sticker next to each word.

ball   leaf

moon   sandwich

Have you got these right?
Then put a star on your reading tree!

Drawing

Draw a picture in the frame
for each word below.

flower   spade   star

Did you draw all three pictures?
Add another star to your reading tree!

Perfect Plurals

A **noun** is a naming word – a person, place, or thing.
A **plural noun** shows there is more than one person,
place, or thing. An "s" at the end of a noun often
means that it is plural.

E.g. shoe – shoes

Circle the plural nouns in the sentences below.

1) They trusted each other completely,
   even with their deepest secrets.
2) A few minutes later, Mouse did the same.
3) They even missed the sad moments.
4) With their arms and legs stretched out,
   they looked just like two furry stars.

Did you get these right?
Then add a star to your reading tree!

Crazy Compound Words

When two short words join together,
they form a **compound word**.

Put the correct word stickers next to the words below to
make a compound word. Then write the new compound
word on the line. We've done the first one for you.

1) every   +   (thing)   = _everything_

2) after   +   = _____

3) any   +   = _____

4) sun   +   = _____

5) with   +   = _____

 Did you get these right? Great!
Then add another star to your reading tree!

Opposite Words

Match the words on the left to their **opposites** on the right. We've done the first one for you.

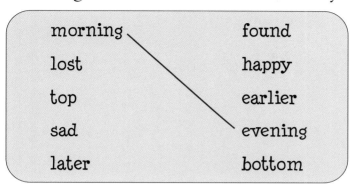

morning   found

lost   happy

top   earlier

sad   evening

later   bottom

Did you match the words with their opposites? Then add a star to your reading tree!

Sentence Order

All stories are made up of **sentences**.
Place the sentences below in the order they appear in the story by adding numbers to the boxes.

☐ Mole and Mouse were the best of friends.

☐ Up and up the hill ran Mole and Mouse, until they reached the top.

☐ They had fun together.

Did you get these right? Remember to add another star to your reading tree.

Neat Nouns

Add the missing nouns to the sentences below
with the word stickers.

days – Mouse – star – summer – Mole – stars

1) "Aren't _____ beautiful?" sighed

Mole happily.

2) But neither found the fallen _____ .

3) _____ and _____ grew

lonely and miserable.

4) The _____ rolled by, and _____

was nearly over.

Did you get all the nouns right?
Add the last star to your reading tree.